FOX ON WHEELS

by Edward Marshall
pictures by James Marshall

DIAL BOOKS FOR YOUNG READERS

NEW YORK

For Darrell Hill

Published by
Dial Books for Young Readers
375 Hudson Street
New York, New York 10014

Printed in Hong Kong by Wing King Tong Company Ltd.

The Dial Easy-to-Read logo is a trademark of
Dial Books for Young Readers,
A Division of Penguin Books USA Inc.,
® TM 1,162,718

Library of Congress Cataloging in Publication Data
Marshall, Edward. Fox on Wheels.
Summary: Fox baby-sits for his sister, Louise, learns to climb
a tree for some grapes, and wins a shopping cart race.
[1. Foxes–Fiction.]
I. Marshall, James, ill. II. Title.
PZ7.M35655Fq 1983 [E] 83-5254
ISBN 0-8037-0001-6
ISBN 0-8037-0002-4 (lib. bdg.)
10 9 8 7 6

The art for each picture consists of a black ink
line-drawing with three overlays reproduced
in red and green halftone and black tint.

Reading Level 1.9

DOCTOR FOX

On Saturday
Carmen called Fox
on the phone.
"Dexter and I are going out
on our skateboards," she said.
"I'll be right over,"
said Fox.

"Not so fast, Fox," said Mom.
"I'm taking the twins to the doctor.
And you must stay with Louise."
"Rats!" said Fox.

"Now, none of that," said Mom.

Fox told his friends
that he could not go out.
"And all because of *you*,"
he said to Louise.

"Now, don't give me any trouble."

Soon Fox was lost
in his TV programs.

He did not give Louise
another thought.

All of a sudden
there was a loud crash.

It came from the backyard.
"Uh-oh," said Fox.

Louise had taken a bad spill.

"Oh my gosh!" cried Fox.

"Louise is dead!"

But Louise was not dead.

"Help!" said a tiny voice.

"Get me out of here!"

Fox was very upset.
"It's all my fault," he said.
"It's all my fault!"

"I want to go to my room,"
said Louise.
"Of course," said Fox.

"I want to lie down," said Louise.

"Of course," said Fox.

"I need soft music," said Louise.

"Of course," said Fox.

"Make a tuna sandwich," said Louise.

"Of course," said Fox.

"Read me a story," said Louise.

"I'll be glad to," said Fox.

“Are you feeling better?” said Fox.

“Not much,” said Louise.

“What can I do now?” said Fox.

“Rub my toes,” said Louise.

“Certainly,” said Fox.

“Mmmm,” said Louise.

Just then Louise's friends
Spud and Dora Jean came by.
"Can Louise come out?" they said.
"I'm afraid not," said Fox.
"Louise has had a bad spill."

"Just a minute," said Louise.

And she hopped right out of bed.
"I'm much better now," she said.
And she ran outside to play.

"Hmmm," said Fox.

FOX AND THE GRAPES

One day Fox was riding his bike
in the park.
"Gosh," he said.
"This makes me really hungry."
Just then, something fell
out of a tall tree.
It was a grape.
"That's odd," said Fox.
"Grapes don't grow on trees."

"Hi," said a voice.
Fox looked up
and saw Millie.
She was eating
a bunch of grapes.
"I love grapes," said Fox.
"Want some?" said Millie.
"Yes, please," said Fox.

"Come on up," said Millie.
"Uh," said Fox.

Fox didn't like high places.
Not one little bit.
"Just drop some down,"
he said.

“Oh, no,” said Millie.

“You have to come up.”

“Uh,” said Fox.

“You aren’t afraid, are you?” said Millie.

“Of course not!” said Fox.

"Then climb up,"
said Millie.
"All right," said Fox.
"Here I come."
Fox took a deep breath.
He closed his eyes.
And he started
to climb the tall tree.

But he made a serious mistake.
He opened his eyes
and he looked down.

"Oooh," he said.
"I'm so high up!"

And he climbed back down.
"What's the matter?"
said Millie.

"Nothing," said Fox.
"I'll be right up."

He tried again.
But he came back down
this time too.
"I thought you weren't scared,"
said Millie.
"I'm not," said Fox.
"I just don't want
any grapes after all.
They're probably no good."

Fox went to another part
of the park
and sat down to think.

He was cross with himself.

He really *didn't* want
any grapes now.
But he just *had* to climb that tree!

This time he got a running start.

And this time
he made it all the way
to the top.
"Oh, I'm so glad you're here,"
said Millie.
"I'm scared!
I don't know how to get
down!"

"Well, that's just *dandy*!"
said Fox.

"Want a grape?"
said Millie.

FOX
ON
WHEELS

One Saturday morning
Fox ate breakfast in a hurry.
"I'm off to meet the gang!" he said.
"Hold your horses," said Mom.
"But we're going to have
a bike race!" said Fox.
"You can race later," said Mom.
"I need some help around here."
"Doing what?" said Fox.
"Take your choice," said Mom.
"You can look after Louise.
Or you can go shopping."

TELEP

Fox looked at Louise.

"Too much trouble," he said.

"I'll shop."

"Here is the list," said Mom.

"This will take *all day*!" said Fox.

"Then you must hurry," said Mom.
"And don't forget the tuna fish
for Louise's sandwich."

At the market
Fox ran into the gang.
They had to shop too.
"We'll just have to race later,"
said Fox.
"Too bad," said Dexter.
"I have an idea," said Carmen.
"Why don't we race right now?"
"Great idea!" said her friends.
"Let's race from one end of the store
to the other!" said Fox.
"Fine!" said the gang.

AISLE 9: JUICE

"On your mark, get set, go!"
cried Fox.
And the race was on!

Dexter pulled out ahead.
"Gangway!" he cried.

Suddenly a wheel fell off his cart.

"Nuts!" said Dexter.

"I'm out of the race!"

"Beep, beep!" cried Carmen.

And shoppers ran for their lives.

Carmen was about to win.
But just then her cart
crashed into a barrel of pickles.
"Oh, fudge!" said Carmen.

"Hooray!" cried Fox.
"I won, I won!"

But some of the shoppers
had angry words for Mr. Sloan.
"Shopping here is *dangerous*!"
said nice Mrs. O'Hara.

"It won't happen again,"
said Mr. Sloan.

When Fox got home,
his mom was on the phone.

"Oh, really?" said Mom.
"He didn't!
He *did*?
Well, it won't happen again!"
And she hung up.

"I hear you're the fastest fox on wheels," said Mom.

"You bet I am," said Fox.

"Care to prove it?" said Mom.

"I'll get my bike," said Fox.

"Hold your horses," said Mom.

"I have a better idea."

"Rats!" said Fox.

"These aren't the wheels

I had in mind!"